Nadakkave, Kozhikode, Kerala, India
+91 4954020666 | +91 9400737475
www.insightpublica.com
e-mail: insightpublica@gmail.com
Colour of Love
Hridya KT
(English Stories & Poems)
First Edition: April 2021
Copyright©Reserved

ISBN 978-93-91006-48-8

Colour of Love
Hridya KT

Born on 6th sept 1991 as daughter of KT Gopalan and Pushpalatha.Studied in BEM Girls Higher Secondary School Calicut. Completed Graduation from IHRD Calicut. Completed MTech from Bits Pilani.Working as a senior software engineer in Infopark Kochi.

Brother: Mohith KT

Husband: Amal Vishnu KS

Daughter: Aruvi A H

Contact Details:
Email:hridyakt@gmail.com
Phone: 9497308171
Facebook: https://www.facebook.com/hridya.kt.7
Insta: instagram.com/kthridya

HRIDYA KT

Dedication

Whenever my dreams come true, I never think it's because of my luck, neither of my hard work or because of my potential. It's all because of the sacrifices my parents have done throughout their life protects me and my dreams all along.

Dedicating this book to my beloved parents... accha & Amma...

Preface

I am expressing myself through my writings here... you can see my heart, the path I travelled, the feelings I carried, throughout in this book. Any word which made you to feel empathetic means we found each other... a beautiful feeling where the reader and writer shares the emotions through words...!

There are many things in my life which I achieved... but many of them where for answering the society. But whenever I look inside and think what I have done for myself, sometimes I feel my hands as empty.

But now I feel I can hold this book tightly when I feel void...

Your prayers and love are my strength. Love you all...

CONTENTS

STORIES

LAST SLEEP...

Everyone will have different reasons to like rain. Each rain will have some story to tell us. Sometimes I feel, "why god didn't gave color to rain drops as my tears?". Perhaps God may forget both...,

I have a painful memory regarding rain. I had a cousin brother, his name was Arun. I called him Vavi ettan. We both had an age difference of five years. Since he didn't have own sister, I was his little sister. We always play together, study together, fight together. We both like to enjoy rain.

He likes food very much hence he always feels hungry and he always suffer from stomach ache. He didn't like to take medicine. Whenever his mother gave him medicine, he used to throw it without seeing her.

I used to wake up late always. He wake up first and pour water in my ears to make me wake. Once I got angry and told, "One day I will definitely pour water in your ears".

He replied, "Only if it is my last sleep..."

I still remember after these thirteen years also... It was an evening of April 12, I fought with him for some simple reasons. He

called me, "Hridya, come... it is raining... see how nice it is..."
But without telling a single word, I close the door and slept. But
for the first time he got angry on me and he went to his house. I
was shocked. Whenever we had any fight, he used to come with
chocolates. Sometimes I simply made fight to get those chocolates. I called him several times. But he didn't give any reply. But
I was sure on April 14 he will come, since it is vishu.

April 14 morning, I was sleeping... I felt someone is pulling
my legs. He usually does like this. I slept as I am sleeping. But
I heard a sudden cry. I ran to kitchen, my mother was crying.
I didn't understand anything. We went to his home. There I
saw him sleeping covered with a white cloth. I remembered his
words, "...only if it is my last sleep".

"last sleep..."

I understood, he is no more. The stomach ache he was suffer-
ing from was a swell in pancreas gland and since he didn't take
medicine properly, it affected his liver also. I didn't get him in
phone was because he was in hospital that time. No one told me
this also.

He was taken finally to the place where he used to throw
medicines...

I slept in his room. Even I couldn't cry. I saw his books, color
pencils, toys everything waiting for him, without knowing he
won't come again.

Someone told, "Arun's eyes were open still... he had some
wish when he died"

I didn't tell anyone, that wish was to enjoy rain with his little
sister.

That time also rain was there outside, silently telling his last
wish to me...

MY LOVE STORY!

I don't know how to start this story... as of now I didn't face such a dilemma to portrait anything... if you ask me, how I am related to this love story, I am unanswerable... is this my story... no!... then? but yet I am writing this Love story... this story consist of many feelings in love... fear of love, pain in love, satisfaction in love.. and many more...!

I am inviting you to the college life of Maya. Maya was an innocent girl, she was very sensitive too... anything can make her cry and the same way small things can make her smile also... College life was totally different from school life... school life was so materialistic that students were evaluated on the marks they get... but college life was really a new world for Maya... she found the essence of poems from there...

In an election campaign time... she saw him for the first time, he ask her to vote for his political party... she didn't feel anything special in him... Love at first sight cannot be occur for everyone right! ?

In the Magazine Committee for that year, Maya was also a member... Magazine Editor was the same Person... Amal... the way he edits the articles of others... every stone consists of an idol... he was expert in editing to make everything more beautiful... love towards poems, Maya got attracted with him... an Infatuation every girls may get at some point of their life... they became good friends... later they came to know that they are family friends...

One Sunday Maya was in her driving class, she saw him on the other way.. she waved her hand... Driving sir asked "who is that guy?"

Unknowingly She told, "My cousin, father's brother's son... "

Amal came near, by seeing the driving sir he asked "Maya, is this your Father! ?"

Driving sir stared at Maya... after Amal left, sir asked

"your Cousin don't know your Father! ?"

Maya was not able to see anything Infront of her... she neither heard anything... she was in some other world... "what happened to me...!" She was surprised... a new feeling... her heart started beating in some other rhythm... she loved to hear his name with her name... in her diary pages she simply wrote his name along with her name... a sweet feel of fear to see him doesn't restrict her to be far from him... she herself created situations to meet him...

Next day she went to his class and called his. She described previous days incident.. that how her driving sir teased her Infront of everyone... He laughed as it is a joke... Suddenly his class teacher came and called him... she left the class... She was only able to see his face... magic in his eyes... his smile... poems in his words... "hey what is happening for me..." she started trying to neglect thoughts about him... but... she lost herself somewhere...

The next day he came to her class... called her... he told "my class teacher started teasing me by telling your name. it will be a problem for us... so it will be good to keep distance. "whether someone threw a stone at my heart ?" she controlled her tears...

and at this pain in heart made her understand that she is in love...

Being in love and cannot express it is a beautiful irritation... Maya intentionally went the places were he came, as if she was not aware... But he was always keeping distance and which made her really depressed... on his farewell day she decided to meet him. she went near his class. He was talking with his friends.by seeing Maya he came near and told today is his final day in college. she asked for his contact number. he saved her number in his mobile and took her hand and wrote his number in her hand. she told him to call her daily...

he replied... "I am not calling my lover only daily..,then how can I call you...! and he smiled... Maya was in a shock and she somehow stop herself from crying... and asked about his lover. he asked her to find out... directly she went to the church near by the college... And cried aloud...

He added her name in his friend list and started messaging her. she also replied for every message. Since Maya knows to write poems, Amal asked her to write romantic poems, so that he can send that to his lover. whatever she felt in her mind about him, she sent him, knowing he will forward that to his lover. Amal considered her as his best friend and he always want Maya to suggest the gifts, which he need to gift his lover. Maya was totally confused.. what to do... by seeing her situation, her friends asked her to stop contact. but she was not able to do that... within that time she was in a situation in which she can't forget him... but being a best friend and hearing about his lover 's story made her in a depression. So she decided to disclose everything to him and to say a good bye...

At last, at the end of her patience, she thought of revealing everything. But he was shocked by hearing everything.

He consoled her by saying,

"it is all age problem. don't get stuck to this and loss your studies".and he added "since you can't forget me when we are in contact. Let us keep distance."

she replied "don't get worry of my situation. My Krishna will guide me... bye..."

It took a long time for her to get out of the depression. But she couldn't forget him.whenever anyone ask about lover or marriage she missed him a lot. Whenever she saw lovers she remembered him... She tried a lot to forget him... but each moment made her to think of him...

After four years... from college life she stepped to professional life... everything changed..her appearance... life style... friends... but one thing remained the same... Her first Love... she missed him even more... but she was not having any idea regarding him... where he will be..? what he will be doing... ?

Her parents started searching guy for her... so she thought... till now lord Krishna has given an answer for whatever questions she asked... but why he made her to love him... she thought of saying a final good bye to him... before forgetting him...

At last she sent him a friend request on April 25.He accepted it on April 26. he asked...,

"Still remember me?"

She replied,

"without remembering how I can sent friend request"

As usual, he sent a smiling smiley... he is always like that... that smile won't go from his face... And from his messages also...

She asked "how are you... ? what doing now?"

He replied, "I am good... now working in Cochin..and how are u ?"

She Answered "I am fine... And how is your girlfriend ?"

After a two minute of silence he replied,

"she will be definitely happy.. because tomorrow is her marriage...!"

Maya was unable to type anything...

He asked again.. "shall I ask something..don't feel bad.."

She replied, "no... tell me..."

He typed "you know this before and now you came to tease me right? otherwise how you pinged me on the correct day... after four years... ?"

Tears came from her eyes... again she is the culprit... why Krishna..! Why you are always doing like this... ?

She replied " No... I did not know about this... I am swearing in the name of Krishna..."

He texted.. "ya... I know, you can't hurt anyone... and you can't lie in the name of your Krishna..."

She felt relaxed... Because in these four years of time.., she never tried to contact him only because of the reason it may hurt him... She can't even imagine teasing him...

He texted "Maya.. I am not in a good mood.. Catch u later bye..."

She read the chat again and again.. after long four years his name on her chat list...

But day by day from his chatting she understood, he was in a depression because he had involved a lot in his love... Sometimes some words of him hurt her more and more... But... yet she asked her parents not to search a guy for her now.. After two years of her course only she is ready to get marry...

Maybe she is again ready to wait for him for two more years... She hoped after recovering from this situation, he will start loving her...

Love is a special feeling. The more and more you get hurt.. the more and more you will urged to get love...like a fly coming near the fire knowing it will burn her...!

Slowly a good tone of friendship again came to their relationship... daily they used to share everything happened on that day...

Maya was eagerly waiting for evening..so that he will come online and chat with her. Sometimes her emotions will overflow and she struggled hardly to hide her love...

but love is like a fire..hiding love is like covering fire with a paper... fire can burn the paper... that happened in their love also... everything which she hided for four years burst as tears one day...

Then he asked "Maya... are you sure that you will be happy with me for the entire life... ?what you know about me... ? still why you are loving me? many differences are there between us... above all once I broke your heart badly... I don't think I am deserving your unconditional love... and you remember once my class teacher teased me with your name? that time, I told him you are my best friend and Aishwarya is my loved. He smiled and told, either one of them will remain in your life the other will go... that is the reason that I avoided you from college...

Maya Replied "I don't know to think many things... but I want to follow what my heart says..."

Again Amal told, "since you are small and not matured enough, you can't think many things about life..but there are many things... I am talking from my experience... but one thing I can tell you... you are so special for me... but I can't make you cry anymore..so think well... there are many factors. Your parents, brother... no one should get disappointed because of this decision. I don't want anyone to get disappointed because of me"

Amal gave her three months of time to think on this... so again for three more months they remained as best friends...

Maya thought, "for Long four years, I was thinking on this.. then what more I can think in three months...!"

And they remained as best friends..understanding each other..caring each other...

And finally that day came... for which they were waiting.But these three months were lengthier than those four years... That night 12' O Clock her phone rang... with great excitement she took the phone... in a low voice he asked, "What you decided finally?"

She replied, "I thought of the negative and positives of my decision..."

He asked, "Happy to hear that you are talking as a matured girl... then what is the conclusion?"

She Continued...

"Since I am deciding about my life by my own. Much opposition may come... but if you are there to hold my hands in any difficulties... I will be there as your girl...!"

Amal told," I gave you three months not to test you... but to make you understand these many negatives are there in me... since you admired me from college days. You may not aware of that... when one is admiring the other only positives will be counted. But that is not life. In love negatives also should be loved, should be admired... Now I understood... you were correct... I only was not knowing what is love... I considered your love as immature. Boasting myself from that blind world... Now I know... I am the luckiest guy in this world. God tested me this much to give you... For any reason I won't leave you... Love you dear...!"

Maya closed her eyes tightly to hear those golden words... the whole world was silent for her that time... only his words she heard...!

May be God wrote this story with his own hand... by taking four years he beautified it maximum... Now Amal and Maya is dreaming about their future with the permission and blessing of their parents... J

OUR MOTHER NATURE

In a crowded railway station, where people are running like ants, trains are roaring, shopkeepers shouting "tea Tea... Coffee... Coffee..."

Thomson a gentleman around forty year old is sitting on a bench in the platform. He was in deep thoughts hence was absent-minded about the surroundings.

A professor was sitting on the other edge of the bench. Professor noticed Thomson. By seeing his idle nature Professor came near Thomson and asked, "May I know your good name please?"

"Who are you?" Thomson replied as he is not interested to talk

"Ok... Well I will introduce myself. I am NandaKumar. I am a professor in Literature. May I know your good name please? Anyhow my train is late by an hour. So if you don't mind we can talk for some time. By the way when your train will come?"

"I am not waiting for any train. I came here to sit alone where no one will notice me. I like loneliness more now"

"Oh I think you are in depression. If I can help you please let me know."

"My Name is Thomson Antony. I am working in Government

sector. If you ask me my problem, I don't have anything as such. But I don't know why I am not at all happy in life"

Nandakumar got confused and told" that is strange man"

Thomson continued, "Yeah, I studied well as per my parents wish. I got government job at the age of 20, got married by 25, have two children. I have everything as per society's angle. But believe me I am empty inside"

Nandakumar smiled and replied, "Living to satisfy society is nothing but killing oneself. You will never get satisfaction."

Thomson thought for a while and told" I don't know for what my heart aches for"

"You please listen to the nature instead of society. We all are part of this nature. And thus the nature knows what we want better than us. Nature always tries in bringing that to our hands but all bad conditions are brought by our negative thinking. Please understand nature's language and follow it, you will reach your destiny"

Thomson was confused, "Nature's Language?"

Nandakumar replied, "Yes, Nature has a language. You need to concentrate to understand it through the art of prayer"

Thomson was again confused; "Prayer is an Art?"

Nandakumar explained "of course! By deep core prayer you will realize yourself. Whatever you ask in prayer you will receive."

He continued,

"God is nothing but this nature. Nature has a rhythm and we all are part of it.

Consider an apple on your dining table. You can go and get it through front door, back door or any of the windows of your house, but the apple will be the same. Likewise, if you enter through the door of church, temple or mosque God is one and the same.God is inside you. Make yourself more and more powerful by good deeds and thoughts. So you will be cured"

Thomson argued "Good deeds? I have done many good things in life. Helped many people, have done many donations. still I am unhappy!"

Nandakumar explained,

"Listen brother, have you noticed all big trees will always bend its head downwards, but when it's blossomed with fruits and flowers it will bend more. Nature is teaching us the value of humbleness.

In holy Bible it's mentioned as,

"For those who exalt themselves will be humbled, and those who humble themselves will be exalted"

Be more humble when nice things happen for you. Also you may have helped many people but if you did all these expecting return then it's of no use. Or if you use all these to boost yourself or to showcase yourself it will never give you happiness.

Moral of Bhagavat Gita is

"Do Karma without expecting results"

In Glorious Quran also tells us that,

"Blessed are those who can give without remembering and take without forgetting"

So believe in the eternal beauty of nature. God doesn't want you to be unhappy. Nature is trying its best way to make you happy. Otherwise, you won't get a chance to born in such a nice place. Just listen to the rhythm of nature, concentrate yourself, understand your talents, use every opportunity and live a happy life dear. Life is very beautiful for those who knows how to live."

A new feeling of freshness came in Thomson's face, he replied.

"I got a new feel of self-realization after listening to your words. This conversation will be a U-turn in my life. Thanks a lot Sir"

Nandakumar smiled,

"No need to thank me brother, as I told before nature has seen your worry. So when you called from deep sorrow, I am appointed as a coincidence. You should Thank God for giving such a beautiful life."

Nandakumar walked away saying goodbye.

A train came with rhythmic engine sound and a smoky smile. Nandakumar got on the train. Thomson waved his hand till the train leaves from his eyes.

We all are like Thomson to some extent. We will do everything to answer society's question by forgetting ourselves. But once the shadow will fly breaking this darkness because we all are beloved ones for this Mother Nature.

Thank you...

POEMS

SILENT LOVE

Walking hands in hands,
we walk through the sands!
our footprints sang the song of love!
yet we never heard it!
wind gazed at us!
why idiots are always silent?
yet we remained silent!
our footprints were always aching,
lets always be together!
but cruel wave of fate washed it away!
but when you reached far and turned back,
your eyes were silently weeping,
"I loved you more than you did" &&&
"I missed you more than you did"

●

BEING AWAY

My poems may vanish from
the heart of age!
my love may be far from
your heart...!
may mystery of my mind,
still strange for you!
but with the soul of
my pulse, I am feeling you!
even my tears are weeping,
in search of you!
my poems are sinking
in this tears...!
yet, why can't you feel my love!

●

MY HEART

Sweet Voice Of Ringing Bell Woke Me Up
Suddenly I Realised My
Heart Was Missing...
I Searched All Around!
Someone Knocked At The Window,
I Opened The Window,
I Saw Beautiful Picture Of Nature,
There I Found My Heart!

●

MY MOM!

Like an angel she came to my life,
With her silent patience,
She mould me up!
When i blindly ask her,
"What is love?"
She poured blood from heart,
& Said "this is my love on you"
Sure,life is short!
But mom, my love on you is long!

●

STROKES; HUES AND SKETCHES...

I was sinking in depth of my heart,
In search of essence of a poem...
I asked my heart,what is a poem!
And what is its language!
But my heart sink in itself & said;
"Give strokes of experiences &
Hues of love to me:
And sketch yourself...
That's a poem...!
Oh lord... I was again scared;
I asked my mind,"what's a poem?"
And "which is the most beautiful poem written?"
He smiled and replied,
"When your tears are the strokes,
And your heartblood is the hue of a poem,
And when it sketches an ocean of love,
In you,... It s the greatest poem!11
Yet... I was doubted!
I asked my soul,how to write a nice poem?
It thought for a while and replied;

"When someone strokes your heart-
With his love,make a hue of memories in your mind,
And sketches a unique picture of life in your soul...,
You are the most beautiful poem written by him!
Yes... And now i realised!
Dear... Iam the most beautiful poem sketched in you!

●

ALMIGHTY

Yes! They are holding their hands...
But their believers are Quarrelling in name of them..
Surebelief is not a foolish feeling;
Hence believers cannot be fools!
So be a true believer of the eternal almighty...
As the physical form of love,trust and truth-
Are not important in true relationships,
True feelings can only be feel... Cant be shown!
Likewise the physical image of god is not matter;
But the moral values can be feel... Which will guide us..!

God! Is the physical image of eternal love;
Not a representative of any religion
But the moral support matters...

Both christ and krishna born as poor..
Their sacrifices made them live through ages...
Both were fond of domestic animals
False hands tried to kill both;but...
Truth cant be suppressed,
As fire can't be cover with paper...

Krishna was an ideal personality;
Who was naughty at his mother;
Sweet romantic at his lover;
Noble friend at friends..
And childish at his father..
Also rude at his enemies...

But the same childlike baby,
Who steel ghee from yashoda;
Gave the matured advice to arjuna-
 The great bhaghavat gita
This is personality and not a mask with strong smile
And rough words as we seen in people of these ages

Yes...The great king of dwaraka was
Curious in poor kuchela's food...
Watch, value of people is not when he forget his
Fellow being when he reach at heights...
The purest form of love is radha's tear drop...
But not a world of fantasy as we seen today!
Yes.Meaningful sadness are far better than-
Meaningless happiness...

Jesus!The one who feed many with a little food
Who healed diseases with love and peace...
The only man who can tolerateto,
The one who cheated him,and...
The only man admitted all of our mistakes
And... Prayed for us even when he was hanged!

Sacrifice is the purest form of love...
Believe in god... And make the morals live in you...
Thus feel almighty!And be valuable

●

MY COLLEGE LIFE...

Those days which never came back,
Were most beautiful part in my life!
A world of colours...
A valley of music... .
From where i find mystery of poems..!

Whatever we sang were poems there,
And whatever we sketched where pictures..!

Ihrd... My small college...
Wherewe shared long happiness..,
Fellow sorrows and funny feelings...!

Our teachers were friendly,
From where i got love in depth,
And the essence of knowledge!

My friends were pulse of my soul,
Whose eyes flooded with me-
Even before hearing my sadness...
They cheered up when they finds,
Happiness in me...

They never complained for my mistakes...
But... Admitted it with me,
When iam punished...
Their fellow arguments, stupid quarrels and
Idiotic philosophies were my inspiration in campus...
Their childlike opinions were always my moral guide..

The tears which took my heart,
Are the beads of experiences today..,
The problems which took away my sleep,
Were now fun for laugh.,
Yes... Experiences matters a lot!

Sure college arts was the celebration of colours.,
Our sports was the loudness of sounds...

Our natural trip to wayanad...
Our joyful efforts in NSS camps...
And our cheerful college tour..

Like a little girl wondering at the
Stars at sky.,
I found many experiences which were,
Far better than mere bookish knowledges.
Some of my friends fell in foolish love,
Which gave meaningless happiness at the beginning,
But love in depth may get pained..
But true love is jewel of soul.
True love begets love... But only at the end... .!
Heart of true love seekers must be,
Wide as a sea...
Then only waves can wander... And,
The almighty sun can set..,
But foolish love is like a narrow pool.,

Which only reflects the poor moon...
Thus i learned to be an ocean.,
Waiting for my love sun to set...!

And now after the three years,
Its time to say bye to my beloved college
Who gave me hand full of values,
Mind of experiences and a heart of love!
Dear..Iam still in you., As a small poem...
●

AS STRANGERS...

My eyes where always in search of you...
My heart was always weeping for you...
In the depth of my heart -
You were always with me..!
Your memories gave me strength to live..
But...
Still as strangers we crossed each other..
Even a small smile break the wall!
Up on lord i dont know,
Why i couldn't smile!
Am i so stranger to you?
Was my love so rude to you?
And now my last words for you-
" Please forgive, if my love pained you lot... Bye"

●

INSPIRATION

I wonder! Where i lost my heart!
I searched all around!
Someone knocked the window...
"Hey open... .!I am here...!
I opened the window;
There i found the picture of nature...
Where i found, mist drops inspire by kissing-
Flower buds to say"open your eyes... "

Where moist breeze hugged plants-
To say;"hey come on!Lets dance.."

Where i heared,morning wishes of birds...

Fields gazed at the sun and asked;
"How dare you miss me last night?.."

Rivers flow gently as if,
She is in a curious search!

Waves approach eagerly to kiss the land!
But land avoid it cruely...!

But...
Gentle wind inspire the wave,
"True love never runs smoothly"

From where i got true inspiration..
Yes..., Nature is a wonderful inspiration...
●

IN SEARCH OF THE WAVE...

A gift i got from depth -
Of my sleep is a dream!
Like a tragic movie,
It made me panic!
Waves were roaring at me,
A stranger was going far,
Suddenly,my mother woke me up!
Ofcourse i got angry;but...
Her tears washed away my anger...
I was upset why her eyes were shedding...
We went to my love nest-
Where my cousin lives...
Between crowds i saw him,
Without any naughtiness..,,
Truth came to my heart,
And i realised his death...
Suddenly i realised my dream,
Perhaps the man moving away,
May be my cousin brother!
Still i am searching for the wave-
Which attack him from me!

●

BEING IN A
MAGICAL FEELING...

I wonder till now how I wrote poems about love without
knowing the feeling..!
I was in my dream world seeking the answer for love.
But now you came to my life to give me the answer, and now I
don't know how to write this magical feeling..!
May be this mysterious feeling is called love...!

A sweet fear of hiding this secret is holding me back from writing,
Because now whatever I write, whatever I paint, whichever
song I sing is not about love...,
It's only about u...
Even without talking a word you stayed back yet...
Why you didn't call me in your painful days... ?

But you know one thing dear...
these long years has proved me that
I can't love anyone except you...
One red rose which you are given means me a lot than a
garden of flowers...

Loving one is a special feeling of love...
But cant love anyone else even in your ignorance was a painful
feeling of love...
And now I am enjoying the eternal feeling of those four letters
"LOVE"!

Once you told me that you are a black paper and to stay apart...
But dear I don't want to know your past... And
I am sure that once you will start loving me... but promise me
that
Only my poem should be there in that paper then...
Because I love you so much...

Since you made me alone these many years,
I will take a dark revenge,
Promise me that you will die only after my death...,
then only you will know how badly I missed you...
And more over, I can't miss you anymore in my life...

●

COLOUR OF LOVE...!

You always put yourself in silence...!
Why I didn't realize the rhythm of your heart,
While walking close to you before... ?
You always irritated me by arguing for simple reasons...!

Once I told, "colour of love is red"
U asked:
"can you tolerate red blood flowing from your beloved one?"
I told, "then blue is the colour of love"
Again, you told,
"why blue sky is so far if his love towards earth is so strong?"
You made me confused again... I told
"green is the colour of love"
You argued again'
"every butterfly seeks honey in flowers not in green leaves..."
I got angry and I shouted, "white is the colour of love"
You smiled and told,
"how can you trust moon's love,
its surrounded by many stars right.!? "
This time I lost patience and I shouted,
"why you are always arguing,
I know what is love better than you... "

But dear...
Then I didn't understand the meaning of your smile...!
Now you showed me the colour of love...,
The wonder of care..., the melody in smile...
Dear...,! Without you I am nothing now
First time in life I feel myself as special...
Now I am feeling more colours which I didn't see before...!
colour in your eyes when you look at me
as if you are not seeing...!
colour in your smile when you read my poems and simply
asking,
about whom these poems are...
knowing it's all are about you only...!
And now I understood...
"there is no colour for love!"
Love makes every colour more beautiful...!"
●

A NEW LIGHT...!

A new light... which made me to smile and dream...!
A new friend... a new companion. Who teach me to love...
I am not loving you for the reason what you are,
But for the reason what I am in your presence...!
How all of my day dreams came true through you... ?
How you took my soul in your eyes... ?
Till now, I kept myself in a wall of reserve character...
Everyone knocked it... but you break it...
Now I understood why I was hiding myself...
I was waiting for you...
Now I can see new colours,
Which I didn't seen before...!
Now I can feel new weather,
Which I didn't feel before...!
Now I know why river is flowing to reach ocean,
even struggling all the obstacles...!
Now I understood the reason for sky to cry as rain,
When rainbow vanishes...!
Now I understood why flowers are awaking,
When dew drop kisses...!
Now I understood why moon is alone...!
It is not loneliness, but solitude... waiting for someone special...!

Arrangements for convenience is not love...
Even the solitude for true love is special...,
Which words can't express...!.
And now I understood why sky is blue, rose is red...
And tears are colorless...!
Yes...! Love is reflecting in everything as colours...,
Love is the essence in everything...
and now I can feel the miracle...!
From where all my poems are getting a new rhythm... ?
Ya... all of my poems are hiding something special...
May be this miraculous feeling is called Love...!
Now I came to know, Life is beautiful than dreams...,
For those who know to love...!

●

WHICH YOU NEVER KNOWN...!

I was curious about you in all my dreams...
The thing which I always forget to tell you was nothing but love...
At last you came to say me "good bye",
In the corridor of our college...
And you disclosed your sweet secret-
Which you hide from me till now...
It was about your sweet hearts glittering eyes...
But you didn't see tears glittering in my eyes...
When I walked away with a fake smile by hiding my tears..
You were still dreaming about your lover's glittering eyes..
And now... I am changing myself as a poem about you...
Which you have never known...

●

YOUR HIDDEN SMILE...

Oh Krishna! As Duryodhana, I don't want
your thousands of soldiers who fights for me, but...
As Arjuna I need you to be with me,
with flute in your hand instead of weapons
and your magic smile on your face.
Thus teach me the essence of Geetha
and make me aware of my own Karma...
and make me strong morally to fight for Truth.
make me understand myself in this-
Kurukshetra war of Life...
When I got hurt in my Life,
I thought you were asking me to walk through-
a bridge of thread which I am afraid of...
But now I understood, you were holding me throughout-
Walking along with me...
In my sad times, I thought I am seeing only my footprints-
in this hot desert, feeling myself alone.
But... Now I understood that I was mistaken!
It was your footprints and I was in your caring hands...
So that I didn't get my legs burned...
And now I realize the meaning of your hidden smile...
Now I am feeling myself guilty because,

even without understanding your love -
how badly I scolded you...
But I know the only one who loves me -
more than I did is you Kanna...
So you will never leave me alone...

●

LOVE AS RAIN...!

Love is like a rain...! that will occur in everyone's life...
for some it will come as heavy rain...
And for some as a light rain... for some it will make thunder and lightning...
But is there anyone who never enjoyed this rain?
But this rain occurred in a different way for me...!
Still now my mind was like a dark sky that waits for rain...
I thought this creative irritation is called love...
for these long years, Love was a question for me which didn't got any answer
But now I got the answer through your eyes...
We were far from the time I started loving you...
Yet why my eyes searched for you in every crowd?
Why I can't forget you at least for a second... ?
Why I liked to write my name with you? And why I erased it before seeing by anyone?
Why my eyes silently remembered you whenever anyone talks about love... ?
Till now I wrote poems about you...
But now why I am struggling to get words when you came beside!?
Still now I thought my love for you is most perfect,

But now you proved me love can be more perfect than mine...
How you still remember my poem which I gave you even without,
Expressing my love... ?
yeah but this is a special feel that we are walking beside without expressing each other, but knowing each other well...
But then why you stayed so far till now if you loved me so deep for these many years?
Ya! I am going to take revenge that -
As I know how horrible is to miss you..,
Let death also comes together for us...!
Dear give me a promise that never leave me alone till we die.
Because these many days have proved me that no one can replace you from my life...
Now, as I am getting wet in this rain... each raindrop is whispering your name in my ears...
May this love rain never stop from our life...!

●

RHYTHM OF TWO HEARTS...

It's a beautiful stage of life,
When you have rhythm of two hearts inside you...!

Yeah, it can be a pretty fellow as per her father's wish,
Or can be a naughty one as per my wish.

I wonder of the days when I scared on this period,
Even in my deep core prayer, I asked "why all pain for girls? "

Perhaps, I was blind at the beauty of this pain!
As all teenage girls, thoughts came to my mind,
"Your tummy which you maintain by hard exercise became size
of a pumpkin,
Face like an aunty, legs bulges as elephant, have medicines than
food, missed your diet chart,
Put on weight like your head fitted over a mountain edge"

As all immature girls,
I also liked freedom to wander whole world,
chit chat with friends,
Like a butterfly with wings,
I flied without boundaries

Thousands of questions kicked my head,
How the baby will be like,
Whether S/he will listen me,
What to do when S/he cries,
How to take care the new one,
when I don't know to take care myself
Whether I can be a good mom,
as I know it's such a responsible role

But slowly on top of all anxieties,
I wished to see his/her face
I started loving my new friend,
Who disturbs my sleep by kicking me from inside?
S/he became my favorite reason to lose sleep

Once tears came in my mind,
When my partner asked
"Why God didn't made a strategy that,
Husband can also share half of the pain? "

He cared me like a parent,
Bared my temper, gave everything I wished for.

And that day came we eagerly waited for,
On the peak of every pain, I prayed
"Give me all the pain Lord,
But make sure my baby is safe"

And thus my second heart came out from me,
As a pretty baby girl with dimple on her right cheeks...

When I gave her to her father,
I understood meaning of life,
Thus she made me a Mom
●